Riddles for Kids

*Creative Riddles, Puns, and
Knock Knock Jokes for Smart
Kids – And The Entire Family
(Ages 5 to 15)*

Annabelle Erikson

Table of Contents

Don't forget,
if you like my book,
or even if you don't,
I want to hear about it!
I encouraged you to leave
A review on Amazon.
Help others decide to buy!

Introduction

If you are looking for a fun time, lots of laughs and giggles, then you have picked up the right book! Jokes are a universal way to connect with friends and family and share a laugh. In fact, we connect more over laughs than anything else. Besides, who doesn't love that rumbly feeling in our tummies when we laugh? Kids often tell the funniest jokes we have ever heard and sometimes they need some new material to keep the laughs going. This book is composed of riddles, play on words, and several knock-knock jokes that will have your kid and you rolling in stitches!

Let your kid read this and ask you questions, or read them together and have fun making strangers or family laugh! There is always time for a laugh. I hope that as you read this and learn the jokes that you have a good chuckle yourself. The chapters are devised in such a way that there are age-appropriate jokes in each section, but don't worry! You can learn the jokes from any section they are all safe - and funny! So let's get knocking!

Chapter One: Riddles and Jokes for Ages 5-8

By now you are probably telling a lot of great jokes! Your funny bone should be in full swing. Let us take a look at some funny knock knock jokes, puns, and riddles that you can add to your list! You can read this book with family or on your own; whichever way you prefer is just fine.

You can have lots of fun asking mom and dad different knock knock jokes, or better yet! Ask them a riddle. All the answers are at the back of the book, but take a chance to see how easy it is for you to get the answer without peeking! Sometimes you might even make up your own answers that fit the riddles. The great thing about a joke is that it is meant to be shared!

So, get out there, get joking and get laughing. This chapter introduces you to some knock knock jokes, puns, and even riddles. Some you may have heard before, others might be new. Hopefully your belly rumbles with laughs as you read and share them.

Knock Knock Jokes[1]

Knock, knock.
Who's there?
Cauliflower?
Cauliflower who?
Cauliflower doesn't have a last name, silly.

Knock, knock.
Who's there?
Amish.
Amish who?
Really? You don't look like a shoe!

Knock, knock.
Who's there?
Wooden shoe.
Wooden shoe who?
Wooden shoe like to hear another joke?

Knock, knock.
Who's there?
Boo.
Boo who?
Why are you crying?

---

[1] knock knock jokes are universal, and many have been around for hundreds of years, so these jokes are common and can be found in other places too. The great thing about this compilation is that all the best ones are in one place!

Knock, knock.
Who's there?
Harry.
Harry who?
Harry up and answer the door!

Knock, knock.
Who's there?
Hatch.
Hatch who?
Bless you!

Knock, knock.
Who's there?
Cash.
Cash who?
No thanks, but if you have one I'll take a peanut!

Knock, knock.
Who's there?
Canoe.
Canoe who?
Canoe come out and play with me?

Knock, knock.
Who's there?
Big interrupting cow.
Big interrupting cow who?

MOOOOOOO! (You say this part while the other person is in the middle of asking their "who" question. That's what makes this joke a hoot!)

Knock, knock.
Who's there?
Lettuce.
Lettuce who?
Lettuce in, it's cold out here!

Knock, knock.
Who's there?
Ice cream.
Ice cream who?
Ice cream, you scream!

Knock, knock.
Who's there?
I am.
I am who?
You don't know who you are?

Knock, knock.
Who's there?
Ya.
Ya who?
 No, I prefer google.

Knock, knock.
Who's there?
Nonya.
Nonya who?
Nonya your business!

Knock, knock.
Who's there?
Banana.
Banana who?

Knock, knock.
Who's there?
Banana.
Banana who? (repeat this part of the joke a few more times)

Knock, knock.
Who's there?
Orange.
Orange who?
Orange you glad I didn't say banana?

Knock, knock.
Who's there?
Justin.
Justin who?
Justin the neighborhood and thought I'd visit!

Knock, knock.
Who's there?
Alpaca.
Alpaca who?
Alpaca the suitcase, you pack the car!

Knock, knock.
Who's there?
Tank.
Tank who?
You're welcome!

Knock, knock.
Who's there?
Cargo.
Cargo who?
Car go honk honk!

Knock, knock.
Who's there?
Leaf.
Leaf who?
Leaf me alone.

Knock, knock.
Who's there?
Isabel.
Isabel who?
Isabel working, I had to knock.

Will you remember me one year from now?
Yes.
Will you remember me one month from now?
Yes.
Will you remember me one week from today?
Yes.
Will you remember me one day from now?
Yes.
Knock, knock.
Who's there?
See, you already forgot me!

Knock, knock.
Who's there?
Dishes.
Dishes who?
Dishes the police! Open up!

Puns and Play on Words

What happens to a frog's car when it breaks down? It gets toad away.

Why was six scared of seven? Because seven "ate" nine.

Can a kangaroo jump higher than the Empire State Building? Yes, because the Empire State Building can't jump.

How do you count cows? By using a cowculator.

What do you call a bear that has no teeth? A gummy bear.

Why does your nose run, but your feet smell?

How do trees get on the internet? They log on.

What do you get when you cross an elephant and a fish? Swimming trunks

If you spend your day in a well, can you say that your day was well-spent?

What is a cow without a map? Udderly lost.

How many tickles does it take to make an octopus laugh? Ten tickles.

Insect puns bug me.

I am great friends with twenty-five letters of the alphabet. I don't know why.

Yesterday I tried to capture some fog. I mist.

I would tell you a construction joke but I am still working on it.

Have you ever tried to eat a clock? It is time-consuming.

Someone stole my mood ring. I don't know how I feel about it.

What do you call a sleeping dinosaur? A dino-SNORE.

What did the first plate say to the second plate? Dinner is on me!

What is hairy, brown, and wears sunglasses? A coconut that is on vacation!

Riddles

1. What two keys cannot open any kind of door?

2. They come out at night without being looked for and they disappear in the day without being stolen. What are they?

3. What gets wet as it dries?

4. I have to be broken before you can use me, what am I?

5. What did the one wall say to the other wall?

6. What five letter word is shorter when you add two letters onto it?

7. What do you call an alligator who wears a vest?

8. How do cows stay entertained?

9. I have a neck, but I have no head. What am I?

10. What is yours but other people use it more than you?

11. What comes once in a minute, twice in a moment, but never once in a thousand years?

12. What weighs more, one pound of feathers or one pound of bricks?

13. I can run but I cannot walk. What am I?

14. I never ask any questions but I am always answered. What am I?

15. Why are ghosts bad liars?

16. What has many holes but it can still hold water?

17. Say "racecar backwards"

18. Everyone has one of these, and no one can lose it. What am I?

19. What is big, loud, has four wheels, and flies?

20. I am often heard, but never seen. I only speak when I am spoken to. What am I?

21. There are six children and three dogs, and none of them were under the umbrella. So, why didn't they get wet?

22. There was a man who owned a fox, a goose, and a barrel of corn. He needed to cross the river but his boat only had enough space for himself and one other object. So, he had to take each thing across one at a time, but he could not leave the fox alone with the goose or the goose alone with the corn. How does he get everyone over to the other side?

23. What never gets wetter no matter how hard or how long it rains?

24. I have a mouth, but I do not eat. I have a bank but I have no money. I have a bed but I never sleep, and I wave yet I have no hands. What am I?

25. What is in the middle of America?

26. There were ten copycats sitting on a log. One jumped down. How many copycats were left sitting on the log?

27. What is the longest word in the English language?

28. I have a head, and I have a tail but I have no body. What am I?

29. If the red house is on the right, and the green house is on the left where is the white house?

30. I am round and I can travel both up and down. You can throw me or catch me. I can break windows. What am I?

31. I am round and hot and I live in the sky. When the night falls I disappear. What am I?

32. I am red, blood pumps through me and I live in your chest. What am I?

33. I can be red or green and I am round. I make a tasty snack but you should not eat my seeds. What am I?

34. I do not have eyes, ears, or hands. I am strong enough to move the dirt of the earth. What am I?

35. I am small and yellow and heavy when there are many of me. But when heat is applied I expand and grow large, and I become much lighter. What am I?

36. I have two wheels and two legs. My legs only touch the ground when I am not moving. What am I?

37. When you first get me I am black. I turn red when you use me and I am white when you are done with me. What am I?

38. I can grow long or short, I can be round or square. I can have color or be left bare. What am I?

39. I carry people all day long, they push buttons to tell me where to go. I close when no one is inside me and I wait to be summoned. What am I?

40. I can come in many different colors and sizes. I can be curvy or straight, I can be placed anywhere but I only have one perfect fit. What am I?

41. When you take off your clothes, I put my clothes on. When you take off my clothes, you put your clothes on. What am I?

42. When you look through me I show you things, I sound like only one letter but I am spelled using three letters. What am I?

43. The faster that you run, the harder you will find it to catch me. What am I?

44. I have rivers and streams but I have no water, I have forests but I have no trees. I have cities and towns but I have no people. What am I?

45. I am shaped like a ring, but I am as flat as a leaf. I have two eyes, sometime four but I still cannot see. What am I?

46. I cover your whole body, yet you cannot wear me. The more that you use me the thinner I become. What am I?

47. I can rise up and I can fall down without ever moving. What am I?

48. Most animals have me. Every human has me. I am also found in a book. What am I?

49. I only come to you when you sleep. I might seem real but I am never there when you wake up. What am I?

50. You can throw me far and you can throw me wide but I will always return if I am thrown just right. What am I?

51. I sit in a corner but I travel the whole world. What am I?

52. I stand tall on one leg and I have three eyes. One eye is red, one eye is yellow and one eye is green. If you don't obey me you might find yourself in trouble. What am I?

53. People are always trying to get rid of me, I can not be thrown but I am often caught. What am I?

54. I am never seen, but you are the one who makes me. What am I?

55. I can be long or short. I can be curly or straight. I can come in ordinary colors or painted like the rainbow. What am I?

56. You can find me once in the morning and twice in the afternoon; but you will never find me in the evening. What am I?

57. Every morning I lose my head, but by the evening I find my head again. What am I?

58. If I drink water I will die, but when I eat I grow strong. What am I?

59. When I am unripe I am green, when I am ripe I am red. I can be turned into a condiment or put on your burger. What am I?

60. I am red and have green hair. My seeds are on my outside. I make a tasty treat or a yummy milkshake. What am I?

61. Why did the bicycle not stand up?

62. What happens when you throw a bunch of books into the ocean?

63. Why did the man take his clock to a vet?

64. What would you call a boomerang that never came back?

65. What is faster, the heat or cold?

66. Why did the chicken end up in jail?

67. What did the first mouse say to the second mouse who was trying to steal his cheese?

68. Why was the math book constantly worried?

69. What has two legs but is unable to walk?

70. What vegetable should never be invited on a boat trip?

71. Why did the horse chew with an open mouth?

72. What school supply is the king in the classroom?

73. What would you give a sick lemon?

74. What is a tornado's favorite game?

75. What is a frog's favorite game?

76. What is the potato's least favorite day of the week?

77. What dies but was never alive?

78. What is Count Dracula's favorite fruit?

79. What would you call a seagull that flew over the bay?

80. Where would a witch park her vehicle?

81. What do you do if you are a fan of Count Dracula?

82. What is a witch's favorite subject in school?

83. What makes a skeleton laugh?

84. How did Benjamin Franklin feel when he had discovered electricity?

85. After he fell, who did the monster ask to kiss his scrape?

86. What do you get when you cross a teacher with a vampire?

87. Why did the Cyclops stop teaching?

88. What falls in winter, is cold but never gets hurt?

89. What is brown, round in shape and sneaks around the kitchen?

90. Why did the student keep his trumpet in the freezer?

91. What is the difference between the regular alphabet and the christmas alphabet?

92. Why did Count Dracula have no friends?

93. What do gymnasts, bananas, and acrobats all share in common?

94. Where did the witch have to go when she was naughty?

95. What did the turkey say before it got roasted?

96. What is a ghost's favorite room in a house?

97. What does a skeleton have for dinner?

98. What monster makes the best dance partner?

99. Which side of the turkey has the most feathers?

100.   Why did the skeleton cross the road?

Chapter Two: Riddles and Jokes for Ages 9-12

Jokes are not just meant for young children, but preteens too! As we grow and mature so does our humor and our understanding of the world. This is why jokes will change as we change. I think that everyone deserves a chance to laugh and that is why this book is broken up into sections! As you enter the world of the preteen, take a glance at these jokes. Share them with family, or better yet put your friends in stitches while they laugh. I promise you that you can find a joke they have not heard of yet!

Knock Knock Jokes

Knock Knock!
Who's there?
Beef.
Beef who?
Before I get cold out here, let me in!

Knock Knock!
Who's there?
Beats.
Beats who?
Beats me!

Knock Knock!
Who's there?
Cheese.
Cheese who?
Cheese a great gal!

Knock Knock!
Who's there?
Donut!
Donut who?
Donut know until you open the door!

Knock Knock!
Who's there?
Orange.
Orange who?
Orange you going to open this door?

Knock Knock!
Who's there?
Barbie.
Barbie who?
Barbecue chicken!

Knock Knock!
Who's there?
Caesar.
Caesar who?
Caesar quick, she is getting away!

Knock Knock!
Who's there?
A herd.
A herd who?
A herd you were home!

Knock Knock!
Who's there?
Goat.
Goat who?
Goat to the door to find out!

Knock Knock!
Who's there?
Honeybee.
Honeybee who?
 Honeybee a dear and open the door.

Knock Knock!
Who's there?
Rough.
Rough who?
Rough, Rough Rough! It is a dog.

Knock Knock!
Who's there?
Who.
Who who?
Who who who it's an owl!

Knock Knock!
Who's there?
Some bunny.
Some bunny who?
Some bunny loves you!

Knock Knock!
Who's there?
Amish.
Amish who?
I miss you too!

Knock Knock!
Who's there?
Bed.
Bed who?
Bed you don't know who I am!

Knock Knock!
Who's there?
Comb.
Comb who?
Comb on out and I'll tell you!

Knock Knock!
Who's there?
Dozen.
Dozen who?
Dozen you want to come out with me?

Knock Knock!
Who's there?
Little old lady.
Little old lady who?
Wow! I didn't know you could yodel like that!

Knock Knock!
Who's there?
Needle.
Needle who?
Needle help getting past this door!

Knock Knock!
Who's there?
Radio.
Radio who?
Radio not here I come!

Knock Knock!
Who's there?
Water.
Water who?
Water you doing inside my room?

Knock Knock!
Who's there?
Howard.
Howard who?
Howard you doing today?

Knock Knock!
Who's there?
Hal.
Hal who?
Hal's about you open this door?

Knock Knock!
Who's there?
Heart.
Heart who?
Heart to hear you through this closed door.

Knock Knock!
Who's there?
Halibut.
Halibut who?
Halibut this weather today?

Knock Knock!
Who's there?
Heywood
Heywood who?
Heywood you open this door please?

Knock Knock!
Who's there?
Havanna
Havanna who?
Havanna come in please.

Knock Knock!
Who's there?
Sherwood.
Sherwood who?
Sherwood be nice for this door to open.

Knock Knock!
Who's there?
Honeydew.
Honeydew who?
Honeydew your chores before I come through this door.

Knock Knock!
Who's there?
Luke.
Luke who?
Luke here open up this door.

Knock Knock!
Who's there?
Hugh.
Hugh who?
Hugh and I go together like apples and pie.

Knock Knock!
Who's there?
Kisses.
Kisses who?
Kisses can be your lucky day.

Knock Knock!
Who's there?
Ice Cream.
Ice cream who?
Ice cream at the sight of bugs.

Knock Knock!
Who's there?
Iris.
Iris who?
Irish you would open this door.

Knock Knock!
Who's there?
Iguana.
Iguana who?
Iguana be your friend.

Knock Knock!
Who's there?
Irish.
Irish who?
Irish you could come out to play today.

Knock Knock!
Who's there?
Pooch.
Pooch who?
Pooch your shoes outside this door right now.

Knock Knock!
Who's there?
Ivan.
Ivan who?
Ivan to tell you a vampire joke!

Knock Knock!
Who's there?
Jimmy.
Jimmy who?
Jimmy some jam with my bread please.

Puns and Play on Words

What did the paper say to the pencil? Keep writing on!

What does the end of every Birthday look like? The letter Y!

Where do sheep like to go on vacation? The Baaaaaa-hamas

What do ghosts eat the most in summer? I Scream.

What part a fish weighs the most? The scales.

Why did the teacher wear sunglasses to her classroom? Her students were too bright.

Why was the broom late for work? It over-swept.

What happens when you cross a pie and a snake? A pie-thon!

What does bread like to do on its vacation? It loaves around!

What should you do if you get peanut butter on a doorknob? Break out the door jam!

What do elephants use for vacation packing? Their trunks!

What haircut do bees like to get? Buzzzzz cuts.

What do books do in winter? They put on jackets.

What does an evil chicken lay? It lays devilled eggs.

Why are robots never scared? They have nerves of steel!

Riddles

1. You walk into a room and you have a match, a candle, a kerosene lamp, and a fireplace. What do you light first?

2. I am tall when I am young, and short when I am old. What am I?

3. What word begins with E and ends with E, but only has one letter?

4. What thing has hands but cannot clap?

5. There was a single story pink house. In this pink house, there lives a pink fish, a pink person, and a pink cat. Even the computers, chairs, tables, and shower were all pink. Everything in the house was pink. So, what color are the stairs?

6. What comes at the end of a rainbow?

7. What goes up but never comes down?

8. What starts with the letter T, is filled with T, and ends with the letter T?

9. What letter in the alphabet holds the most water?

10. A woman is sitting in her house at night and there are no lights on. There is no candle or lamp to give her light, but she is reading a book. How is she reading?

11. If you draw one line on a piece of paper, how do you make the line longer without touching it again?

12. How many months have twenty-eight days in them?

13. There are four days in a week that start with the letter T. What are they?

14. There is a railroad crossing, watch out for cars. Can you spell that without using any R letters?

15. There were two mothers and two daughters who went out to eat. Each woman only ate one burger, and there were three burgers eaten in total. How is this possible?

16. How many seconds are there in a year?

17. A man was walking outside when it suddenly began to rain. He had no umbrella and no hat either. All of his clothes got soaking wet, but no hair on his head got wet. How is that possible?

18. You are walking across a bridge when you see there is a boat that is full of people, but at the same time, there is not one single person on the boat. How can this be?

19. A cowboy rides into town on Friday and he stays in town for three days. Then, he leaves on Friday. How did he manage to do that?

20. A young boy was taken to the hospital emergency room. The doctor in the emergency room looked at the boy and said, "I cannot operate or treat this boy because he is my son." But the doctor was not the boy's dad, so how could this be?

21. I have keys, but no doors. I let you enter, but you can never leave. I have space, but I have no rooms. What am I?

22. There are three apples in a basket and you take away two. How many apples do you have?

23. Mary's mom has three daughters. One is named Sarah and the other daughter is named Beth. What is the name of the third daughter?

24. Why is Europe like a frying pan?

25. What tree can you carry in your hand?

26. There is an electric train going east at sixty miles per hour. There is also a strong west wind blowing hard. Which way will the train's smoke drift?

27. How can you throw a ball as hard as you possibly can and have it come back to you without having it bounce off of anything else?

28. Hi, my name is Roger. I live on a farm with four other dogs. Their names are Flash, Speedy, Buddy, and Snowy. What is the fifth dog's name?

29. What do 11, 69, and 88 have in common as numbers?

30. I have one eye but I cannot see. What am I?

31. What word looks the same upside down and backwards as it does when it is usually written?

32. Why do birds fly to the south during winter?

33. I am an odd number, but when you take one letter away from me I become even. What number am I?

34. How do dog catchers get paid?

35. A young boy fell down from a twenty-foot ladder. He did not get hurt, not even a scratch. How is this possible?

36. If you use only addition, how can you get the number 1,000 by only adding together eight number 8s?

37. What does the following word structure mean: I RIGHT I?

38. Imagine for a moment that you are in a room and it is filling fast with water. There are no windows or doors in this room, so how do you get out?

39. There is a big money box that I own. It is about ten inches wide and 6 inches tall. How many coins can I put in my box so that it is no longer empty?

40. The more of me you take, the more you leave behind. What am I?

41. What invention allows you to see right through a wall?

42. You bake a cake for your grandma and you plan to take it to her home which is across the city. Unfortunately, you live in a city that is infested with trolls. You need to cross eight bridges to get to your grandma's house but each bridge has a troll that requires you to give them half of your cakes. The trolls are nice, however, and they will give you back one of the cakes that you give them each time. So, how many cakes do you need to take with you to make sure that you have two cakes by the time you reach your grandma's house?

43. As you are walking towards St Mary you spot a man who appears to have seven wives. Each wife is holding onto seven bags. Each bag has seven cats in it and each cat had seven kittens. Of all the wives, cats and kittens, how many were going to St Mary?

44. What is broken if it is not kept?

45. Did you hear the joke about the roof?

46. I have one head, one foot, and four legs. What am I?

47. How do you spell "cold" by using only two letters?

48. If you are running a race and you overtake the person that is in second place, what place will you be in?

49. How many letters are there in the alphabet.

50. What word in the English language has double letters that appear consecutively three times in a row?

51. What is the center of gravity?

52. I get larger and larger the more that you take away from me. What am I?

53. The turtle took three sweets to Texas in order to teach Trent how to tie his boots. How many T's are in that?

54. I am brown with a head and a tail but I have no legs. What am I?

55. How can you spell rotten by only using two letters?

56. I have two hands and I like to run, but no matter how far I run I always stay in place.

57. I go up but I can never come down. What am I?

58. My name starts with a P and it ends in an E and has over a million letters in it. What am I?

59. How many peas does a pint have?

60. What did one ocean say to the other ocean?

61. What word is spelt incorrectly in every single dictionary?

62. I have many keys yet I cannot open any door. People use my keys and produce melodies. What am I?

63. How can monsters tell their fortunes?

64. What do you get when you cross a vampire and a snowman?

65. What do witches like to order at hotels?

66. Where do ghosts go for a swim?

67. What do birds like to do on Halloween?

68. What smells the best at Thanksgiving?

69. What kind of weather do turkeys like?

70. Why could the turkey not eat dessert?

71. What do elves learn in school?

72. Why was the turkey arrested?

73. Is leftover turkey good for your health?

74. What type of diet did the snowman start?

75. What type of key is the most important key for Thanksgiving dinner?

76. What did the snowman eat for breakfast?

77. What happened to the guy who stole a calendar from the shop?

78. What do you get when you cross an apple and a pine tree?

79. What does Santa use to clean his sleigh?

80. What does December have that no other month has?

81. What did the stamp say to the envelope?

82. Why was Santa's elf sad?

83. What kind of flower do you hope to never get on Valentine's day?

84. What did the paperclip tell the magnet?

85. What is easy to get into but hard to get yourself out of?

86. What has an eye but cannot see and likes to cause destruction?

87. What do elephants tell each other on Valentine's Day?

88. What did the baker tell his wife?

89. Why is the forest so loud?

90. What did the monster ask his crush?

91. What did the squirrel give his friends for Valentine's Day?

92. What did the farmer give his wife for her birthday?

93. What would you call two birds in love?

94. What did the calculator say to the other calculator on their anniversary?

95. Why did the boy bring his ladder into school?

96. What do turkeys get a lot of when they play baseball?

97. What is the best way to talk to a T-Rex?

98. What did the boy pickle say to the girl pickle?

99. Where do pencils go on vacation?

100. Why can skeletons not play music?

Chapter Three: Riddles and Jokes for Ages 13-15

Jokes and riddles are not just meant for little children. Teenagers have a blast with them too! The older you get, the more sophisticated you are going to want your jokes to be; just remember that sometimes the best jokes come from the simplest places.

If you are looking for the perfect joke to make your friends laugh, or even just a good chuckle on your own then this is the perfect chapter for you!

Knock Knock Jokes

Knock Knock!
Who's there?
Sea.
Sea who?
Sea you later alligator.

Knock, Knock
Who's there?
Deer.
Deer who?
I Deer you to open the door!

Knock Knock!
Who's there?
Zombies.
Zombies who?
Zombies are endangered, protect them to protect the flowers!

Knock knock!
Who's there?
Tea.
Tea who?
Tea you later alligator.

Knock knock!
Who's there?
Thailand.
Thailand who?
Thailand me some money please?

Knock knock!
Who's there?
Juicy.
Juicy who?
Juicy that cat stuck in the tree?

Knock knock!
Who's there?
Cameron.
Cameron who?
Cameron, take one, and scene!

Knock knock!
Who's there?
Al.
Al who?
Al clean up if you open this door.

Knock knock!
Who's there?
Atlas.
Atlas who?
Atlas! The door is finally open.

Knock knock!
Who's there?
Alec.
Alec who?
Alec to move it, move it!

Knock knock!
Who's there?
Bea.
Bea who?
Will you Bea my valentine?

Knock knock!
Who's there?
Cupid.
Cupid who?
Cupid open this door please.

Knock knock!
Who's there?
Egg.
Egg who?
Eggcited to start this new day!

Knock knock!
Who's there?
Cue.
Cue who?
Cue the romance, will you be my valentine?

Knock knock!
Who's there?
Eileen.
Eileen who?
Eileen against this doorframe.

Knock knock!
Who's there?
Frank.
Frank who?
Frank you it's nice to meet you.

Knock knock!
Who's there?
Emma.
Emma who?
Emma hoping today will be a sunny day.

Knock knock!
Who's there?
Felix.
Felix who?
I felix-ited about valentines day!

Knock knock!
Who's there?
Fangs.
Fangs who?
Fangs for inviting me in.

Knock knock!
Who's there?
Fonda.
Fonda who?
I'm fonda you!

Knock knock!
Who's there?
Fiddle.
Fiddle who?
Fiddle me, fiddle you, fiddley doo.

Knock knock!
Who's there?
Ghana.
Ghana who?
Are you ghana eat that or not?

Knock knock!
Who's there?
Fran.
Fran who?
Frandship can be a beautiful thing!

Knock knock!
Who's there?
Holmes.
Holmes who?
Holmes is where the heart stays.

Knock Knock!
Who's there?
Value.
Value who?
Value go to the prom with me?

Knock Knock!
Who's there?
Robin.
Robin who?
I'm robin you.

Knock Knock!
Who's there?
Zoo.
Zoo who?
Zoo you like Count Dracula?

Knock Knock!
Who's there?
Stopwatch.
Stopwatch who?
Stopwatch you're doing, it's hammertime!

Knock Knock!
Who's there?
Tank.
Tank who?
Oh, you're welcome.

Knock Knock!
Who's there?
Mustache.
Mustache who?
Mustache you a question about last night, but I can shave it for later.

Knock Knock!
Who's there?
Ya.
Ya who?
Yahoo! We get to see each other.

Knock Knock!
Who's there?
I smell mop.
I smell mop who?
Gross...

Knock Knock!
Who's there?
Voodoo.
Voodoo who?
Voodoo you think you are talking to me?

Knock Knock!
Who's there?
I eat mop.
I eat mop who?
That's too much information buddy.

Knock Knock!
Who's there?
Candice.
Candice who?
Candice house have any more doors?

Knock Knock!
Who's there?
Annie.
Annie who?
Annie way this day can go faster.

Knock Knock!
Who's there?
Howl.
Howl who?
Howl you get through this door?

Knock Knock!
Who's there?
Mikey.
Mikey who?
Mikey broke, do you have a copy for me?

Knock Knock!
Who's there?
Spell.
Spell who?
Fine, It is spelled W-H-O.

Knock Knock!
Who's there?
Dewey.
Dewey who?
Dewey have to do this homework?

Knock Knock!
Who's there?
To.
To who?
Actually, the correct way to say it is "To Whom.

Knock Knock!
Who's there?
Razor.
Razor who?
Razor hands in the air like you just don't care.

Knock Knock!
Who's there?
Dwayne.
Dwayne who?
Dwayne the water out of the sink please.

Knock Knock!
Who's there?
Snow.
Snow who?
Snow use asking me, you already know!

Knock Knock!
Who's there?
Alec.
Alec who?
Alec-t your next president wisely.

Knock Knock!
Who's there?
Says.
Says who?
Says me, that is who!

Knock Knock!
Who's there?
Some.
Some who?
Someday we can be together again.

Knock Knock!
Who's there?
Iran?
Iran who?
Iran all this way to tell you I love you.

Knock Knock!
Who's there?
Stupid.
Stupid who?
Stupid door won't open for me.

Knock Knock!
Who's there?
Amos.
Amos who?
A mosquito just bit me!

Knock Knock!
Who's there?
Euripides.
Euripides who?
Euripides shirts you buy them.

Knock Knock!
Who's there?
Water.
Water who?
Water you waiting for, it's cold out here!

Knock Knock!
Who's there?
Thermos.
Thermos who?
Thermos be an easier way to speak to you.

Knock Knock!
Who's there?
Dozen.
Dozen who?
Dozen anyone want to be my friend?

Puns and Play on Words

What do you do if there is a kidnapping at high school? You wake him up.

My Labrador slipped her collar, but I didn't have to retriever.

I was looking for the lightning when it struck me.

When the bottle of pop hit me, I didn't cry. It was a soft drink.

Why did the teacher send the kid to detention? He swore he did his homework.

What did the Buddhist say to the hot dog vendor? "Make me one with everything"

Why do you never see an elephant hiding in a tree? Because they're great at hiding.

What is red in color and smells just the same as blue paint? Red paint.

A man that is dyslexic walks into a bra.

Where does the Captain rest his armies? Inside his sleevies!

Why are Koalas not considered real bears? They failed to meet the koalafications.

A grizzly bear walks into a sandwich shop and goes: "Can I have a…. grilled….. cheese sandwich please." The water looks at him and asks "Why the pause?" The bear says "I'm a bear, what do you mean what's with the paws?!"

What is a bear with no ears called? A B.

Why do you never see blind people skydiving? Because their dogs would be too scared!

I walked into a pet shop looking for a fish. I asked them if I can buy one of their goldfish. The man asked me if I wanted an aquarium. I had to tell him that I didn't care what the fish's star sign was!

I once saw a wine connoisseur eating grapes. I walked up to him and told him he had to wait a little longer.

What does a pepper do when it gets mad? It will get jalapeno face!

What do you get when you have a dyslexic who is an insomniac who is also an agnostic? A person that lays awake in the middle of the night wondering if there really is a dog.

Two goldfish share a tank. The one fish looks at the other and asks: "So, do you know how to drive this thing?!"

Two marines are in a tank together. The first marine looks at the second and blows water bubbles.

What is brown in color and sticky? A stick.

What is a foot long and very slippery? A slipper.

My friend gave me an epipen while he was dying. It seemed super important for me to have it so I cherish it always.

I am a scarecrow and I have won many awards. People say I am outstanding my field of work. I always tell them: "Hay, it's all in my jeans."

A troubled man walks into a lawyer's office and asks him how much he charges. The lawyer tells him that he charges one thousand dollars to answer three questions at a time. The man who is outraged says: "That's super expensive, don't you think so?" The lawyer counters with, "Yes it is, so what's your third question?"

How did the hipster burn his tongue? He took a bite from the pizza before it was cool.

A man is walking through the desert with a dog and a horse. The dog suddenly says, "I cannot do this anymore! I must have water." The man in astonishment says, "I had no idea that dogs could speak!" The horse says, "Me either!"

Three friends walk into a bar, an atheist, a vegan, and a crossfitter. I know they did because they told me.

What is the difference between a rectal thermometer and an oral thermometer? The taste.

I told my friend a total of ten jokes trying to get her to laugh. Unfortunately, not pun in ten did.

I stayed up all night to try and find out where the sun was coming from. Suddenly, it dawned on me.

What can you not hear a pterodactyl go to the restroom? It's P is silent.

How does NASA organize their parties? They planet.

Have you heard about corduroy pillows? They seem to be making headlines.

What is the pirate's favorite letter? People always think its R, but it really be the C.

Don't criticize a person until you have walked a mile in their shoes. This way, you will be a mile away and have their shoes when you finally do criticize them.

What did the grape that was green say to the grape that was purple? Oh my gosh, you're turning purple! Breathe!

What did the right eye say to the left eye? Between us, something here smells.

What do Winnie the Pooh and Alexander the Great have in common? They both have the same middle name!

Why did the cowgirl get a wiener dog? She wanted to get along little doggie.

Sometimes I tuck my knees into my chest and lean backward. That's just the way I roll.

Why do you not see Giraffes in middle school? Because they're all in high school!

How many freshman do you need to change a lightbulb? Zero! It's a sophomore class.

Why would a middle schooler need to climb a ladder? To get into the high school!

Why did the freshman boy eat his homework? Because he was told it was a piece of cake!

What would you call the leader of an AP biology gang? The Nucleus

Why is it a bad idea to do calculate homework during a party? Because drinking and deriving is a bad idea!

What do you get when you mix your junior year with AP classes? Depression.

Why was the geometry book crying? Because it had too many problems!

Name a bus that you can't go inside? A syllabus!

Why did the freshman have a wet report card? It was below the C level.

Why did the teenager skip the pirate movie? It was rated Arrrrrrr!

Why do we have to do homework? Because it doesn't know how to do itself!

Riddles

1. You have all the water that you need at your disposal and one five-gallon bucket, and a second three-gallon bucket. You need to fill the five-gallon bucket with exactly four gallons of water. How do you do this?

2. Paul is six feet tall. He is an assistant in a butcher's shop and he wears a size ten in shoes. What does he weigh?

3. You are a bus driver. At your first stop, four people get on. Your second stop you have ten people get on. At your third stop, two people get off. At your fourth stop, one person gets on. When you stop for the fifth time everyone gets off your bus. What is the color of the bus driver's eyes?

4. What always ends everything?

5. Madam, Civic, Eye, and Level all have one thing in common. What is that?

6. I am an insect. The first part of my name is the name for another insect that likes flowers. What am I?

7. When you have me you want to share me, but if you share me then you no longer have me. What am I?

8. You can hold me without having to use your hands, fingers, or arms. What am I?

9. The person that makes me has no need for me. The person that buys me will never use me. The person that uses me does not know that they are using me. What am I?

10. The letter T and an island have one thing in common. What is it?

11. Complete this ten letter sequence o,t,t,f,f,s,s ….

12. I am a word in the English language with nine letters, but I remain a word no matter how many letters you take away from me. What am I?

13. I am at the beginning of eternity to the end of time and space. I am at the beginning of every end and at the end of every place. What am I?

14. I am unknown until I am measured, yet when it seems as if I have flown you begin to miss me. What am I?

15. I am where yesterday can follow today but tomorrow is in the middle. What am I?

16. What is black, white, and red all over?

17. I am the thing that man loves more than life, and fears more than death and pain. The poor have me, and the rich need me. Men that are content desire me. A frugal person spends me, but the saver saves me. Every man will take me to their grave. What am I?

18. How much is the answer to this question.

19. I am not a bird, yet I fly. I eat fruit and insects. I sleep when it is light, and I embody darkness. What am I?

20. I stand when I sit, and when I walk I jump from place to place. I have a pouch on my stomach. What am I?

21. You cannot eat me, yet I am the same size as an apple. I am round in shape and yellow in color. I often get hit and thrown around. What am I?

22. Why did the period make the comma stop?

23. I have brown skin, but I am white on the inside. My skin is covered in hair, but you can drink my juice and eat my flesh. What am I?

24. I am considered a special and romantic day. People like to buy flowers and give gifts when I come around. What am I?

25. I represent every country in the world and I am often found in different colors. The wind carries me in its breeze, and I am often found on poles. What am I?

26. I can be made of paper and plastic and I am found in every town. People use me to upgrade their lives. What am I?

27. There are three stoves in a room. A wood stove, a gas stove, and a brick stove. You only have one match. Which do you light first?

28. I am considered a sport where you wear gloves on your hands. Often you do not need a shirt, but shorts

are required. You run around and are held in a ring. What am I?

29. I am done everyday by almost everyone. You must bend your legs in order to do me properly. I am faster than a crawl but slower than a run. What am I?

30. I am a mammal that is found in Africa, and I have both the very first and the very last alphabet letters in my name. I look like a horse but I am not one. Stripes cover my body. What am I?

31. I am like bread, but not bread. I like to be hot and butter can be spread on me. I am normally found on your breakfast plate. What am I?

32. I never was but I am always going to be. No one has ever seen me and no one ever will see me. I give confidence to the world that better times will come. What am I?

33. You can find me in a mine, but I am most often held captive in a case made from wood. Everybody uses me. What am I?

34. I am lighter than a feather, but you cannot hold me for longer than five minutes. What am I?

35. I am a green house, but inside my house there is a smaller white house. Inside the white house there is a red house. The red house had lots of black cats living in it. What am I?

36. I am considered a pest, yet I am only hungry too. I fly around your windows and I flock to the tables for meals. I have wings but I am not a bird. What am I?

37. Why was the teacher unable to control her pupils?

38. What did the French teacher say to her class?

39. In the very beginning of the world, four brothers were born. The first brother could run and never get tired, the second brother always ate but he never seemed to get full. The third brother drank a lot but remained thirty. The last brother was always singing songs and his voice could get loud. What were the brothers called?

40. What do a judge and an English teacher have in common?

41. Where do a biology and chemistry teacher sit when they go to the bar?

42. What book do you not get credit for reading at school?

43. Why do history teachers hate teaching about the middle ages?

44. What is the difference between the SAT and the ACT?

45. What stays sharp if you use it but dull if you do not use it?

46. What do a plant and a school have in common?

47. Why did the selfie end up in jail?

48. What does a jury and a high school basketball team have in common?

49. What did the high schoolers say to one another?

50. What did the punching bag tell the boxer?

51. There was once a poor man who was feeling pretty low at a bar. A man that is sitting next to him and considers himself rich pulls out a wallet that is filled with money. This catches the poor man's attention and he strikes up a conversation with the rich man. He tells him that he knows every single song in existence. The rich man blows him off until the poor man bets him every dollar in his wallet that he can sing him a song with the woman's name of his choice. Finally, the rich man bites and asks the poor man to sing a song using his wife's name: Alda May. That night the rich man went home a poor man and the poor man went home counting the rich man's dollars. What song did he sing?

52. There was once a kingdom that could not be entered without proper papers. The citizens of this kingdom were never allowed to leave once they were inside. One man did not like this rule and he wanted to leave the kingdom, but the only way in or out was on a bridge that took nine minutes to cross. The king had ordered that an archer check on the bridge every five minutes. The man walked across the bridge and made it out of the kingdom without harming himself or anyone else. How did he do it?

53. What did the owl tell his sweetheart?

54. How do you catch a one of a kind rabbit?

55. What did the first piece of string say to the second piece of string?

56. Why did the elephant cross the road?

57. What kind of music do mummies love to dance to?

58. Where can you learn to make ice cream?

59. What would you call an elephant that is in a phone booth?

60. How did the hairdresser manage to win the race?

61. What is a scarecrow's favorite fruit?

62. What flowers talk the most?

63. What did the circle tell the triangle?

64. What is black and white over and over and over again?

65. Why was the music teacher most sought after for everyone's baseball teams?

66. What do spiders love to do on computers?

67. What time is it when your tooth hurts?

68. Why do eggs hate jokes?

69. What is the smartest bug around?

70. Why was the clown crying?

Conclusion

Are you in stitches yet?

Riddles and jokes are often the best way to shake loose the stress of the day and bond with our friends and families. I hope that through reading this book you have found joy and laughter, and maybe even brought some joy to others! There is nothing quite like sharing a laugh. You can keep this book and read it as many times as you need a laugh. You could even commit the jokes to memory and become the joker of your family!

Better yet, you can pass me on to someone else so that the circle of laughter is never broken. I hope you enjoyed reading this as much as I enjoyed putting it together for you. From me to you,

Happy laughing!

Don't forget,
if you like my book,
or even if you don't,
I want to hear about it!
I encouraged you to leave
A review on Amazon.
Help others decide to buy!

Answers

Don't worry! You don't have to try and find the answers to all the questions I asked you on your own. Use this handy answer guide whenever you are stumped and you will find the answer to your riddle! Each chapter has a link that will take you directly to where you want to go! Have fun and happy riddling!

Chapter One Riddle Answers
1. Monkey and Donkey
2. The stars
3. A towel
4. An egg
5. They say "I will meet you at the corner."
6. Short
7. Investigator
8. They go to the moo-vies
9. A bottle.
10. Your name
11. The letter M
12. Neither is heavier! They both weigh the same because they are both a pound.
13. A drop of water.
14. A doorbell.
15. Because you can see right through them.
16. A sponge
17. Racecar Backwards
18. A shadow
19. A garbage truck
20. An echo
21. They were not wet because it was not raining.

22. The man will first take the goose in his boat across the river. Then he will go back and fetch the fox. When he leaves the fox at one end of the river he will take the goose back with him. Then he leaves the goose and brings the corn over so that the fox and the corn are together. He will then go back one last time to fetch the goose.
23. The sea.
24. The river.
25. The letter R
26. No one would be left sitting on the log because they would all follow the first person who got up - because they are copycats.
27. Smiles because there is a mile between the beginning of the word and the end.
28. A coin
29. Washington D.C
30. A ball
31. The sun
32. Your heart.
33. An apple
34. An earthworm
35. Popcorn
36. A wheelbarrow.
37. Charcoal
38. Fingernails
39. An elevator
40. A puzzle piece.
41. A clothes hanger.
42. An eye
43. Breath
44. A map
45. A button

46. A bar of soap
47. The temperature.
48. A spine.
49. A dream
50. A boomerang.
51. A stamp
52. A traffic light
53. A cold
54. Noise
55. Hair
56. The letter O
57. A pillow
58. Fire
59. A tomato
60. A strawberry
61. Because it was two-tired
62. A title wave
63. It had ticks
64. A stick
65. Heat is faster because you can catch a cold
66. He was using fowl language.
67. That's nacho cheese
68. It had too many problems.
69. A pair of pants.
70. A leek.
71. He had bad stable manners.
72. The ruler.
73. Lemon-aid.
74. Twister.
75. Hopscotch.
76. Fry-day.
77. A battery.
78. Neck-tarines.

79. A bagel.
80. In the broom closet.
81. Join his fang club.
82. Spelling.
83. When his funny bone is tickled.
84. He felt shocked.
85. His mummy.
86. You get lots of blood tests.
87. He only had one pupil.
88. Snow.
89. Mince spies.
90. He liked cool music.
91. The Christmas alphabet has noel.
92. He was a pain in the neck.
93. They can all do splits.
94. To her broom.
95. I am stuffed!
96. The living room.
97. Spare ribs.
98. The boogie man.
99. The outside of the bird!
100. To get to the body shop.

Chapter Two Riddle Answers
1. The Match
2. A candle
3. Envelope
4. A clock
5. There are no stairs because it is a single story home.
6. The Letter W
7. Your age
8. A teapot

9. C
10. The woman is blind, she is reading braille.
11. You need to draw a shorter line next to the original line to make it longer.
12. All twelve months.
13. There is Tuesday, Thursday, Tomorrow, and Today
14. T-H-A-T
15. There were only three women. A grandmother, a mother, and a daughter.
16. Twelve. January 2nd, February 2nd, March 2nd, April 2nd, May 2nd...
17. The man was bald.
18. All of the people on the boat were married.
19. The cowboy's horse was named Friday.
20. The doctor was his mother.
21. A keyboard
22. You would have two apples if you took two apples.
23. Mary is the third daughter's name
24. It is similar to a frying pan because it has Greece at the bottom.
25. A palm tree
26. There would be no smoke because electric chains don't blow out smoke.
27. You would throw the ball straight up in the air.
28. Roger is the fifth dog's name.
29. The numbers read the same if they are right side up or even upside down.
30. A needle.
31. SWIMS
32. It is too far to walk.
33. Seven - if you take away one letter (the letter S) it then becomes even.
34. They get paid by the pound

35. He didn't hurt himself because he fell off of the first rung.
36. You add together eight 8s like: 888+88+8+8+8 = 1,000
37. It means "right between the eyes"
38. You stop imagining.
39. You just need to put one coin in the box for it to no longer be empty.
40. Footprints.
41. A window
42. You need to take only two cakes with you! If you only take two then you only have to give each troll one cake because one is half of two. And if the trolls give you one cake back with each meeting then they never take a cake away from you!
43. Only you since you were the one walking toward St Mary!
44. A promise
45. Over your head
46. A bed
47. IC (ICY)
48. You would be in second place.
49. There are eleven letters in the words "the alphabet."
50. Bookkeeper
51. The letter V
52. A hole
53. There are two T's in the word THAT
54. A penny
55. DK (decay)
56. A clock
57. Your age
58. Post Office

59. There is one P in pint.
60. Nothing, they waved at one another.
61. Incorrectly.
62. A piano
63. They read their horror-scopes.
64. Frostbite
65. Broom service
66. The dead sea
67. They go trick or tweeting.
68. Your nose
69. Fowl weather.
70. He was stuffed.
71. The elf-abet.
72. It was suspected of fowl play.
73. Not if you are the turkey!
74. The meltdown diet.
75. The tur-key
76. Frosted flakes.
77. He got twelve months.
78. Pine-apple.
79. Comet.
80. The letter D
81. I am stuck on you!
82. He had low elf-esteem.
83. Cauliflower
84. I find you very attractive.
85. Trouble.
86. Hurricane.
87. I love you a ton!
88. I am dough-nuts about you!
89. Because all the trees have bark.
90. Will you be my valen-slime?
91. Forget me nuts!

92. Hogs and kisses.
93. Tweet hearts.
94. Let me count all the ways that I love you.
95. To get to the high school.
96. Fowl balls.
97. From a distance.
98. You mean a great dill to me!
99. Pencil-vania.
100.   They have no organs.

Chapter Three Answers

1. You fill the five-gallon bucket up with water first and then pour it into the three-gallon bucket. Empty the three-gallon bucket. Pour the remaining two gallons from the five-gallon bucket into the three-gallon bucket. Fill the five-gallon bucket up again and then pour the water from it into the three-gallon bucket. When you are done you should have exactly four gallons left in the five-gallon bucket.
2. He weighs meat.
3. Your eye color because you are the bus driver.
4. The letter G
5. They're called Palindromes. This means that they read the same backwards as they do forwards.
6. Beetle.
7. A secret
8. Your Breath
9. A Coffin
10. They both appear in water.
11. E, N, T. The first letter of each number from the number series from one to ten.

12. Startling is the nine letter word. You start by removing the L which leaves you with Starting. Then you remove the second T which leaves you with Staring. Remove the A and you have string. Take away the R and you are left with Sting. Remove the T and you are left with Sing. Remove the G and you are left with Sin. Take away the S and you have in. Take away the N and you have I which is still considered a word.
13. The letter E
14. Time
15. A dictionary
16. An embarrassed Zebra.
17. Nothing.
18. How much.
19. Bat.
20. A kangaroo.
21. A tennis ball.
22. It was at the end of its sentence.
23. Coconut.
24. Valentine's day.
25. A flag.
26. Paper money.
27. The match is lit first.
28. Boxing
29. Walking
30. A zebra
31. Toast
32. Tomorrow and/or the future.
33. Lead pencil
34. Your breath
35. Watermelon
36. A fly

37. She lost her glasses.
38. I don't know because I couldn't understand her.
39. Water, Earth, Fire, Wind.
40. They both spend their day handing out sentences.
41. A periodic table.
42. Facebook.
43. There are too many knights spent on it.
44. One letter.
45. The brain
46. They both have STEM.
47. It was framed
48. They both go to Court.
49. Nothing. They texted each other.
50. Hit me baby one more time.
51. The poor man sang the happy birthday song.
52. He started crossing the bridge the first five minutes that the archer was gone, and when it came time for the archer to check on the bridge he acted like he was walking back toward the kingdom. When the man failed to provide the proper papers he was sent away from the kingdom.
53. Owl be yours.
54. Unique up on it!
55. Will you be my valen-twine?
56. It was the chicken's day off.
57. Wrap music
58. Sundae school
59. Stuck
60. She knew a shortcut
61. Strawberries
62. Tulips, because they have two lips.
63. I don't see your point!

64. A penguin rolling down a hill.
65. The music teacher had the perfect pitch.
66. They like to make websites.
67. Tooth hurty.
68. They crack up.
69. The spelling bee.
70. Because it broke his funny bone.

References

Some of these jokes and riddles are originally created, and others are famous through time. You will be able to find a few of these riddles in other places, but not so many or so great as a place like this

Made in the USA
Middletown, DE
23 January 2020